Dedication

Dedicated to the cat: Mister Pudge
In memory of the cat: Spooky

I am forever grateful to my family for their inspiration, support, and love. My family complete me: my husband Jim, daughter Maureen with her husband Brian and their baby daughter Laurel, and son Michael with his wife Kim. My family encourage me to make my dreams realities. As an educator I have always supported children in the writing process and the journey to publication. Now it is my turn.

www.trafford.com

North America & international
toll-free: 1 888 232 4444 (USA & Canada)
phone: 250 383 6864 ♦ fax: 250 383 6804
email: info@trafford.com

The United Kingdom & Europe
phone: +44 (0)1865 487 395 ♦ local rate: 0845 230 9601
facsimile: +44 (0)1865 481 507 ♦ email: info.uk@trafford.com

10 9 8 7 6 5 4 3 2

Mister Pudge

By Kathleen A. McMahon

Illustrated by James P. McMahon

Mary and Marty Bright were a happily married couple. They lived in a warm climate. Their home included a beautiful spacious backyard with a big tree and a long fence. Cats felt comfortable there. They would run around climbing the fence and the tree.

The sky was blue without a cloud.
The sun was bright and warm.
The grass was fresh and green.
A kitten was born in this backyard.
Its fur was splashed with black and white.
What a beautiful sight!

Sometimes Mary would place water and kitten food on her porch.
The scent of cat food made the kitten excited and delighted.

Mary and Marty decided to name this kitten
"Mister Pudge." He became the center of their lives.

However, there was never enough kitten food for all the outside cats and kittens. Mister Pudge met other cats who fought and clawed him. He got scratched and hurt. He became thirsty, hungry, and unhappy.

Mister Pudge always stayed in the pretty backyard, which was his birthplace. It felt like his home, a place where he never felt alone.

From inside the house Mary and Marty watched
Mister Pudge each day. He came to their home and
refused to budge. He was always at their door.
They grew to love him more and more.

The kitten meowed: "I look in. What do I see? A happy home where I want to be."

One day Mister Pudge was at their door with a cry. The couple
opened the door to learn if this kitten wanted to live inside their
home. He did and now the kitten no longer had to roam.

The couple made certain his water bowl was always
filled and fed the kitten the tastiest food. Mister
Pudge ate, played and grew. He was in a joyful mood.

This cat could be chatty with lots to say. "Meow, meow, meow," he welcomed each new day.

The couple wanted to make their cat happy. He had always climbed the tree outside. They bought him a tall cat playground with high places to climb and sit.

Mister Pudge could view the entire outside with a happy meow: "I look out. What can I see? Other cats... Stay away from me!"

Mister Pudge enjoyed jumping up and down. He was a strong cat. He could reach high places, even if he had to land in small spaces.

He did not like any other cats to come into his special space. Mister Pudge meowed: "I look out. What can I see? Other cats. Stay away from me!" He was the only household cat, and that was certainly a fact.

Some of the windows would be opened for Mister Pudge to rest. He would sit so still as he peered through the glass checking the grass. He looked out every window. He appeared to guard the family and home like a "watch cat."

At night the couple would go into their bedroom to sleep. Mister Pudge would sleep with them each night.

Mister Pudge had a toy mouse he chased all around the house. He also had a toy which would make him jump so high, almost reaching for the sky.

To brush was to pet. To pet was to love. The couple
brushed Mister Pudge with love.

Mister Pudge was most content in his new inside
world. He felt safe and loved. He became a "watch cat."
From this home, he would never scat.

Mary and Marty Bright and Mister Pudge were now a happy family. Now the outside cat looking in was an inside cat looking out.